KT-525-979

2008.
Molly Mae's
1st Christmas

Nana & Grandpa
x x

LITTLE MISS
Story Treasury

Roger Hargreaves

EGMONT

We bring stories to life

MR.MEN   LITTLE MISS

MR. MEN and LITTLE MISS™& © THOIP (a Chorion Company)

Little Miss Story Treasury © 2008 THOIP (a Chorion Company)
Created by Roger Hargreaves and Adam Hargreaves
Designed by Sheryl Bone

This edition published in 2008 by Dean,
an imprint of Egmont UK Limited
239 Kensington High Street
London W8 6SA

ISBN 978 0 6035 6373 7
3 5 7 9 10 8 6 4 2
Printed in Italy

All rights reserved. No part of this publication may be reproduced,
stored in a retrieval system, or transmitted, in any form or by any means
electronic, mechanical, photocopying, recording or otherwise,
without the prior permission of the publisher and copyright owner.

Roger Hargreaves' Little Misses are loved by children across the world. This unique treasury features everyone's favourite characters in some amusing and entertaining adventures!

The stories are easy to read aloud to younger children, as well as being very appealing to older readers.

This book belongs to

....

....

LITTLE MISS
Story Treasury
Roger Hargreaves

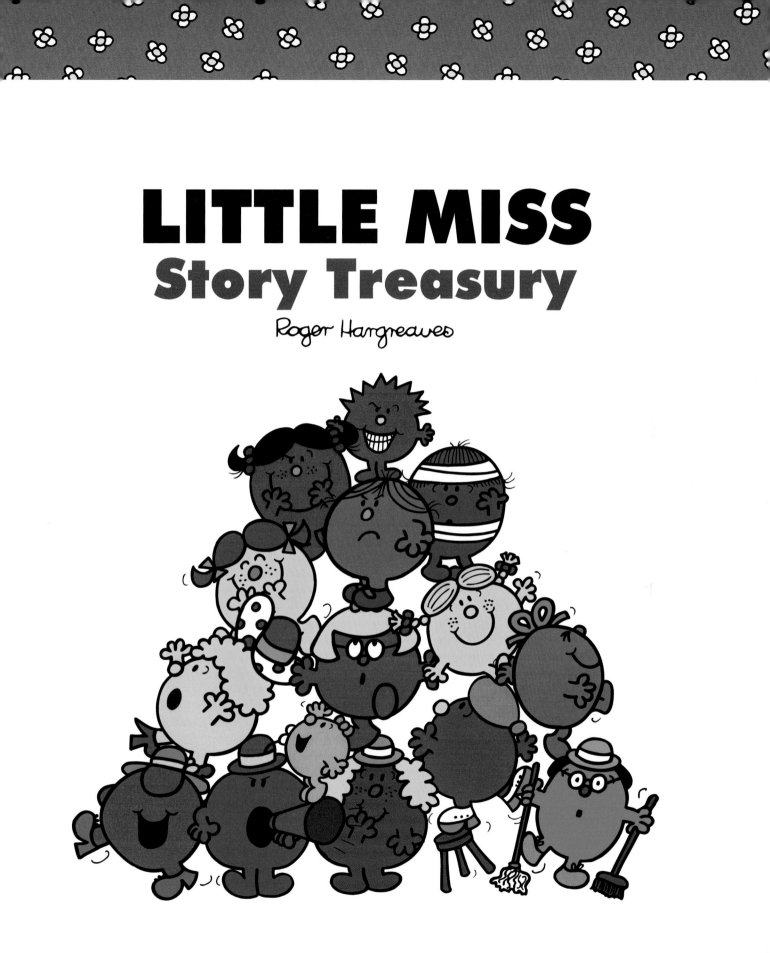

CONTENTS

LITTLE MISS SUNSHINE
keeps her smile

Little Miss Sunshine and Mr Grumpy
couldn't be more different.
Can Mr Grumpy succeed in
changing Little Miss Sunshine?

Little Miss Sunshine lives in Rise and Shine Cottage on the bank of a river.

And Little Miss Sunshine, as her name suggests, is a very happy person.

The sort of person who never gets in a bad mood.

The sort of person who is the exact opposite of somebody else who appears in this story.

That somebody is Mr Grumpy.

And Mr Grumpy, as his name suggests, is the grumpiest person in the world.

The sort of person who is always in a bad mood.

Everything annoys him.

Flowers growing in his garden, sunny days . . . and rainy days. But the thing that puts Mr Grumpy in the worst possible mood is seeing other people being happy.

10

One morning, Mr Grumpy met Little Miss Sunshine.

"Good morning, Mr Grumpy," said Little Miss Sunshine, cheerfully.

"There is nothing good about it," snapped Mr Grumpy.

"Humph," huffed Mr Grumpy, after Little Miss Sunshine had left.
"That Little Miss Sunshine is always so abominably happy!
Just for once I'd like to see her in a bad mood."

11

It was on his way home that Mr Grumpy thought of a plan. A plan to upset Little Miss Sunshine.

He raced home and made a list of all the things that were guaranteed to upset him.

It was a very long list!

"Now, there must be something here that will put Little Miss Sunshine in a bad mood," he said to himself.

Mr Grumpy was not a very nice man!

The first thing Mr Grumpy had written on his list was, 'waiting for buses'.

So the next day Mr Grumpy opened a gate and let all Farmer Field's sheep out into the lane! And the bus was delayed for hours and hours while all the sheep were rounded up.

Mr Grumpy ran round to the bus stop.

"Tee hee," he chuckled nastily, "I can't wait to see how upset Little Miss Sunshine is."

But Little Miss Sunshine was not upset. In fact she was not at the bus stop at all.

As it was such a nice day, she had decided to walk into town.

"Bother!" said Mr Grumpy.

13

The next day, Mr Grumpy looked at the second thing on the list.

"Losing," he read out loud.

So that evening he invited Little Miss Sunshine round to his house to play cards and . . . he cheated!

But Little Miss Sunshine being the happy-go-lucky person she is, did not mind losing.

Mr Grumpy won every game they played.

"Oh, well played Mr Grumpy," she said, at the end of the evening.

"Bother, bother," said Mr Grumpy after she had left.

Mr Grumpy read down his list again.

Number three said, 'getting caught in the rain'.

Mr Grumpy filled up his watering can and, using his ladder, climbed a tree just outside Little Miss Sunshine's house.

And there he waited until Little Miss Sunshine came out for her walk.

But Little Miss Sunshine saw the ladder.

"What a silly place to leave a ladder," she said to herself, and walked round the other side of the tree and put the ladder away.

"Bother, bother, bother," muttered Mr Grumpy, who ended up stuck in the tree all night.

Well, nearly all night. Just before sunrise he fell asleep . . . and fell out of the tree!

The fourth thing on Mr Grumpy's list was 'queues'.

Mr Grumpy waited until Little Miss Sunshine went shopping. Then he rushed ahead of her to the greengrocer's, where he started an argument with Mrs Pod about the quality of her peas.

As he argued, a queue began to grow behind him and when he glanced back, he saw Little Miss Sunshine standing at the end of the queue.

He smiled to himself and carried on arguing until he felt sure she must be fed up of waiting.

But when he turned around, the queue had disappeared. When he went outside, he found everyone in the queue happily chatting with Little Miss Sunshine.

"Double bother, bother!" he said.

Mr Grumpy was furious.

But then he met Mr Nosey and had another thoroughly nasty idea.

"Do you know," said Mr Grumpy, "what Little Miss Sunshine calls Little Miss Bossy behind her back? She calls her knobbly knees!"

Mr Grumpy's thoroughly nasty idea was to start a rumour that would get Little Miss Sunshine into trouble.

And the rumour spread.

Mr Nosey told Little Miss Star who told Mr Uppity who told Little Miss Splendid who told . . . Mr Muddle . . . who told Little Miss Bossy.

". . . and Little Miss Sunshine said that Mr Grumpy calls you knobbly knees," said Mr Muddle.

"Did he now!" said Little Miss Bossy, grimly, and marched straight round to Mr Grumpy's house and punched him on the nose!

It was a very sorry-looking Mr Grumpy that Little Miss Sunshine met outside her house the next day.

Little Miss Sunshine invited him in for breakfast to cheer him up and cooked him fried eggs. Sunny side up of course!

And did she manage to cheer up Mr Grumpy?

Of course not!

No more than Mr Grumpy can upset Little Miss Sunshine!

LITTLE MISS TROUBLE
moving house

Little Miss Trouble is lonely because
she doesn't have any neighbours.
Find out what happens when different
people try living next door to her!

Little Miss Trouble lives in Uptonogood Cottage surrounded by fields and trees and more fields and more trees, and even more fields.

Her nearest neighbours live miles and miles away and there is a very good reason for this.

That very good reason is Little Miss Trouble!

Nobody wants to live next door to somebody who causes so much trouble.

Somebody who telephoned Mr Lazy at 5 o'clock every morning for a whole week.

And somebody who told Mr Wrong that the best thing to use to polish his car was boot polish!

Now, because she lived all on her own, Little Miss Trouble found that she could not cause half as much trouble as she would like to.

What she longed for more than anything else was a neighbour.

One Monday, when Little Miss Trouble was walking in the woods near her house, she found a wishing well.

"Well, I never," she said, and then she had an idea. She threw a coin in to the well.

"I wish I lived next door to . . . somebody," she said out loud.

Later that day, when she looked out of her window, she discovered that as if by magic, which it was, her house was next door to Box Cottage, which is where Mr Chatterbox lives.

"Tee hee, now for some fun!" giggled Little Miss Trouble.

She crept down the lane, around the corner, up a telegraph pole and cut the telephone line!

Poor Mr Chatterbox.

No telephone.

No one to chat to.

But it was then that he looked out of the window and saw Little Miss Trouble's house.

Five minutes later, there was a knock at Little Miss Trouble's door.

"Hello," said Mr Chatterbox. "Just thought I'd pop round for a quick chat. A funny thing happened, my telephone's broken and . . ."

And Mr Chatterbox talked and chatted and chatted and talked through the morning, all afternoon and late into the night.

The next day, Tuesday, a very tired Little Miss Trouble went back to the wishing well and threw in another coin. "I wish that I lived next door to someone else," she said.

And the very next morning, Little Miss Trouble found herself living next door to Mr Bump.

She threw a brick through one of his windows to wake him up, but Mr Bump has so many accidents that he did not notice one more broken window.

Little Miss Trouble went back to the wishing well.

On Wednesday, Little Miss Trouble discovered that Little Miss Lucky is too lucky for any of Little Miss Trouble's tricks to work on her!

On Thursday, there was nobody in at Little Miss Late's house.

She was late getting back from her holiday!

On Friday, Little Miss Trouble told Mr Muddle that Mr Small had called him an egg-head.

But Mr Muddle got muddled up and instead of being angry with Mr Small, he thanked him!

On Saturday, Little Miss Trouble let the tyres down on Mr Forgetful's car.

But Mr Forgetful forgot he had a car so he caught the bus instead.

On Sunday, it was a very fed up Little Miss Trouble who returned to the wishing well to make a wish.

And then she had a thought.

A thought that went like this, "The trouble with neighbours," thought Little Miss Trouble, "is that they are too much trouble!"

And she went home and was very, very good and didn't make any trouble for anybody forever and ever . . .

. . . well, not until the next Tuesday!

LITTLE MISS SCATTERBRAIN
sets off for the sun

Little Miss Scatterbrain's friends help
her plan a holiday in the sun.
What could possibly go wrong?

Little Miss Scatterbrain

is the sort of person who gets everything mixed up.

Like the morning she hung slices of bread from the washing line and put her handkerchiefs in the bread bin!

Like the afternoon she vacuumed the lawn and mowed the carpets!

And like the evening when she wanted to watch her favourite television programme, but turned on the radio instead.

Little Miss Scatterbrain is so scatterbrained that she forgets where her own front door is! Have you ever heard of anything so scatterbrained?

This story is about the time that she went on her summer holiday.

Little Miss Scatterbrain, as you can imagine, is not very good at organising holidays.

The year before last, she went skiing, but ended up on the beach!

And last year she went camping and packed an electric kettle!

This time, she was determined that nothing would go wrong.

And to make sure that nothing did go wrong, she asked her friends to help her.

Mr Clever helped to book her summer holiday.

Little Miss Splendid helped her shop for her holiday.

Little Miss Tidy helped her pack.

Mr Rush took her to the station.

And Mr Strong carried her luggage on to the train.

Nothing could go wrong. Or that's what Little Miss Scatterbrain thought.

However, something did go wrong.

And that something was Little Miss Scatterbrain getting off at the wrong station.

She crossed the road and went into the hotel opposite the station.

"Good morning," she said, even though it was the afternoon, "my name is Little Miss Scatterbrain."

The hotel manager looked down his list of guests, but there was no booking in her name. And of course there wouldn't be.

Little Miss Scatterbrain was in the wrong town. And because she was in the wrong town, she had to be in the wrong hotel.

"That's odd," she said, as she came out of the hotel. "Never mind, I'll go down to the beach."

She asked the next person she met where the beach was.

"Sorry, there's no beach here," came the reply.

"That's odd," she said, for the second time that day.

As she stood in the street wondering what to do, somebody else walked by and said, "Looks like snow."

Little Miss Scatterbrain looked up at the sky and as she did so, a large snowflake floated down and landed on her nose.

"That's odd," she said, for the third time that day.

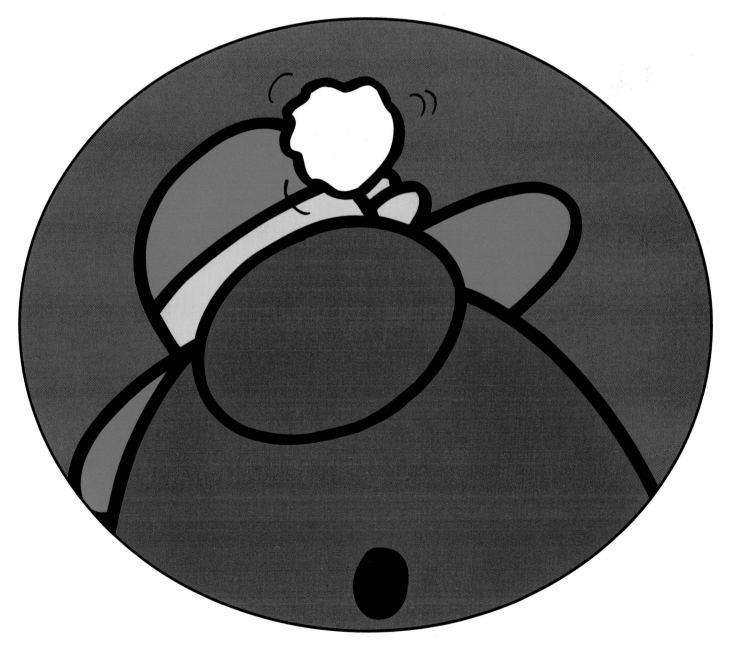

A week later, back from her holiday, Little Miss Scatterbrain met Mr Clever.

"Hello," said Mr Clever. "Did you enjoy your holiday?"

"Yes," said Little Miss Scatterbrain, "do you want to see my photos?" And she showed him her holiday snaps.

Not surprisingly, Mr Clever was rather surprised.

"That's odd. Where did you go?" he asked.

"It began with an 'S'," she replied.
"I know. I booked it for you," said Mr Clever. "You went to Seatown."

"No," said Little Miss Scatterbrain, "hmm, let me think, oh I know, it was Shivertown!"

"I should have guessed," smiled Mr Clever.

"By the way, did you get my postcard?" she asked.

"No, but I did get your postcard meant for Little Miss Splendid," chuckled Mr Clever.

"That's odd," said Little Miss Scatterbrain.

But I don't think there's anything odd about that, do you?

LITTLE MISS BOSSY
and the magic word

Little Miss Bossy is just too bossy!

So Mr Small and Little Miss Magic

decide to teach her a lesson . . .

Little Miss Bossy is bossy.

Bossier than the bossiest person you know.

She is also very rude.

Nearly as rude as Mr Uppity, which is very rude indeed.

She never says, 'please'.

And she never says, 'thank you'.

Like the time she met Mr Sneeze.

"ATISHOO!" sneezed Mr Sneeze.

"Stop sneezing!" ordered Little Miss Bossy.

"I can't, ATISHOO!, help it," replied Mr Sneeze.

"Nonsense!" she replied.

46

Like the time she met Little Miss Chatterbox.

"Good morning," said Little Miss Chatterbox. "Lovely day isn't it? Just the right weather for a walk. Talking about the weather . . ."

"Shut up!" ordered Little Miss Bossy.

And like the time she tripped over Mr Small.

"You're too small!" exclaimed Little Miss Bossy. "Grow up!"

"I can't," said Mr Small.

"Then get out of my way in future!" ordered Little Miss Bossy.

Poor Mr Sneeze.

Poor Little Miss Chatterbox.

And poor Mr Small.

It was Mr Small who decided that something had to be done.

He went to see Little Miss Magic.

And once he had explained the problem, she agreed to teach Little Miss Bossy a lesson.

". . . and I think I know just how to do it," she replied.

The next day, Little Miss Bossy bumped into Mr Greedy.

"You're too big," she cried. "Lose some weight!"

At the same time Little Miss Magic, who had followed Little Miss Bossy, muttered a very magic word.

And do you know what happened?

Of course you don't . . .

. . . but you do now!

"Who are you calling big," laughed Mr Greedy. "You ought to take a look at yourself!"

Little Miss Bossy was lost for words.

As soon as Mr Greedy had gone, Little Miss Magic muttered some more magic words and Little Miss Bossy returned to normal.

Further down the lane, Little Miss Bossy passed Mr Cheerful's gate. He was painting stripes on his house to cheer it up.

"That looks ridiculous," snapped Little Miss Bossy. "Paint over those stripes!"

Little Miss Magic whispered the very magic word again.

Mr Cheerful started to chuckle.

"You ought to look at yourself," he laughed.

Little Miss Bossy did.

She was covered in stripes!

From her hiding place, Little Miss Magic smiled to herself.

Next, she met Little Miss Splendid.

"What a stupid hat," she said. "Go and put on something more sensible!"

Little Miss Magic uttered the magic word again and I'm sure you can guess what happened next.

"Speak for yourself!" said Little Miss Splendid, bursting into laughter.

And for the third time that day, Little Miss Bossy was lost for words.

Just then, Mr Small came along.

"Having a nice day?" he asked.

"Mind your own business, pip-squeak!" snapped Little Miss Bossy.

"And who are you to call me pip-squeak!" said Mr Small and chuckled.

"Haven't you learnt your lesson yet?"

Little Miss Magic came out from behind the bushes and picked up Little Miss Bossy.

"Oh it's you," squeaked Little Miss Bossy. "Turn me back right now!"

"You have to say the magic word," replied Little Miss Magic.

"Abracadabra," squeaked Little Miss Bossy.

"That's not the magic word I was thinking of," said Little Miss Magic.

I'm sure you know what the magic word is, but it took Little Miss Bossy a bit longer to think of it.

"Please," she said eventually.

And did she learn her lesson?

Well, she learnt one lesson.

Little Miss Bossy is still just as bossy as ever,
but at least she now says 'please'!

"GO TO SLEEP! Please."

LITTLE MISS NEAT
and the last leaf

Autumn is a worrying time for
Little Miss Neat! But then along comes
Mr Happy with the perfect solution!

Little Miss Neat likes things to be neat.

Which is why she is called Little Miss Neat.

She likes things to be as neat as two new pins.

Which is why her cottage is called Two Pin Cottage.

One autumn day, Little Miss Neat looked out of her window to admire her neat garden.

As she looked, a leaf fell from the tree in the middle of her lawn.

"Oh goodness gracious!" she cried. "What a mess!"

She rushed outside, picked up the leaf and put it in her rubbish bin.

"That's better," she said to herself, as she went back inside.

But when she looked out of the window again, there was another leaf lying on her immaculate lawn.

Out she rushed again and picked up the leaf and put it in the bin.

And so it went on, all day long.

Rushing backwards and forwards until it was too dark to see anything.

Poor Little Miss Neat was exhausted.

"I don't like autumn," she murmured to herself as she fell asleep.

The next morning was even worse.

Little Miss Neat had to sprint to keep up with the falling leaves.

And that was how Mr Happy found her at lunchtime.

Running backwards and forwards.

"You look exhausted," said Mr Happy.

"I am," puffed Little Miss Neat, "but I have to pick up all these horrid, messy leaves."

"Do you know what I do?" said Mr Happy. "I wait until all the leaves have fallen and then I pick them up. You ought to try it. It's much easier."

62

After Mr Happy had left, Little Miss Neat thought about what he had said and decided she would try it.

But it was easier said than done.

Poor Little Miss Neat paced and fretted and fretted and paced as the leaves slowly covered her lawn.

She hated it.

But eventually, all the leaves had fallen.

Well, nearly all the leaves.

There was just one leaf left on the tree.

Little Miss Neat waited.

And waited.

And waited.

When it got too dark to see, she got a torch and waited.

And waited.

And waited.

All night long!

And that was how Mr Happy found her the next morning.

Still waiting!

"What are you doing?" asked Mr Happy.

"What you suggested I should do," replied Little Miss Neat. "I'm waiting for all the leaves to fall."

Mr Happy smiled, reached up and plucked the last leaf from the tree.

"Oh," said Little Miss Neat, suddenly feeling rather foolish.

And she blushed.

Mr Happy helped her to rake up all the leaves.

By teatime, Little Miss Neat's garden was as neat and as tidy as it usually was.

"You know what you should do next year?" said Mr Happy.

"Oh, please! No more suggestions!" cried Little Miss Neat.

"Don't worry," said Mr Happy "You'll like this one. I think that next year you should go on holiday and ask Mr Busy to clear up the leaves. It wouldn't take him a minute."

"What a good idea!" said Little Miss Neat.

"You've taken a leaf out of my book," smiled Mr Happy.

"And turned over a new leaf," chuckled Little Miss Neat.

"You can leaf through the holiday brochures," giggled Mr Happy.

"And I can leave the leaves behind," laughed Little Miss Neat.

"Hee hee, oh stop it, hee hee hee," laughed Mr Happy.

"Leaf me alone! Ha! Ha! Ha!"

LITTLE MISS NAUGHTY
worries Mr Worry

Little Miss Naughty could have
much more fun if only Mr Worry
would stop worrying her.
But will he spoil her fun forever?

Little Miss Naughty

is quite the naughtiest person that I know.

Take the other day for example.

She tied Mr Tall's shoelaces together.

And she took Mr Dizzy into a maze and left him there.

And she joined up all the dots on Little Miss Dotty's house.

And she even picked on the worm who lives at the bottom of her garden!

I think you would have to agree that she is probably the naughtiest person that you know.

71

Then one day, Little Miss Naughty met Mr Worry.

Now, Mr Worry is the sort of person who worries about everything. Absolutely everything!

"Let's have some fun," suggested Little Miss Naughty, after they had introduced themselves.

Mr Worry was worried that if he said no he might offend Little Miss Naughty, so he said yes.

But he was still worried what 'fun' somebody called Little Miss Naughty might get up to.

And as you have seen, he was right to worry!

Little Miss Naughty led him to Mr Tickle's house.

"Let's ring Mr Tickle's doorbell and run away," she giggled.

"Ooh, I don't know," said Mr Worry. "Mr Tickle might be in the bath."

"Even better!" laughed Little Miss Naughty.

"But then he would be all wet, and he might fall down the stairs, and he might bump his head and then there wouldn't be anybody to call the doctor because we would have run away!"

Up to this point, Little Miss Naughty had never worried about anything in her entire life.

But now, when she thought about what Mr Worry had said, ringing Mr Tickle's doorbell and running away suddenly didn't seem such a good idea after all.

"Come on," she said. "I've got a better idea."

They walked over to Mr Uppity's house.

"Why don't we let his tyres down?" chuckled Little Miss Naughty.

Mr Worry looked worried.

"But what if Mr Uppity didn't notice he had flat tyres until he got out on the road, and then he might get stuck, and then a fire engine might come, and it might not be able to get past, and then it couldn't put out a fire!" gasped Mr Worry.

75

"Oh," said Little Miss Naughty. "I hadn't thought of that."

She had thought of something else though and off they went.

But it didn't matter what she thought up, Mr Worry could think of something to worry about. Which then gave Little Miss Naughty something to worry about.

They didn't push Mr Bounce off the gate because he might have bounced up into a tree and never been able to get down again.

They didn't scatter Little Miss Scatterbrain's marbles because she might have got upset if they had been lost.

Little Miss Naughty was distraught.

All those wonderful, naughty ideas going to waste.

And then she had another idea.

And tripped up Mr Worry who fell flat on his face!

"What did you do that for?" said Mr Worry. "I might have rolled down the hill, and I might have fallen in the river, and then I might have caught a cold, and I might have had to stay in bed all week!"

Little Miss Naughty looked at Mr Worry.

"But you didn't," said Little Miss Naughty,
and ran off, giggling mischievously.

LITTLE MISS DOTTY
has a dotty day out

Little Miss Dotty is about
to have the dottiest day ever in
Nonsenseland – with her dotty
friends, Mr Nonsense and Mr Silly!

Little Miss Dotty

is every bit as dotty as her name suggests.

For instance, last year, Little Miss Dotty carpeted her garden path!

She lives in Nonsenseland, where the grass is blue and the trees are red, a place which is every bit as dotty as Little Miss Dotty.

In Nonsenseland all the pigs have televisions . . .

. . . and wear slippers.

One day, while she was walking through Whoopee wood, she met her two friends, Mr Silly and Mr Nonsense.

"Hello," she said.

"Hello," said Mr Silly and Mr Nonsense at the same time.

Mr Silly was carrying a saw.

"We're going to make a see-saw," said Mr Nonsense. "Would you like to join in?"

"Yes, please," said Little Miss Dotty, who had been wondering what to do.

So the three of them set off.

They walked and they walked and they walked a long, long way until they came to the seaside.

But being Nonsenseland, the sand wasn't yellow, it was pink.

When they got to the water's edge Mr Silly threw the saw in!

Have you ever heard of anything so silly?

"Brilliant," said Mr Nonsense.

"That's the best sea-saw ever," agreed Little Miss Dotty.

"What shall we do now?" said Mr Silly.

"Let's go for a paddle," suggested Little Miss Dotty.

So they went to the shop on the pier and each bought a paddle!

"That was fun," said Mr Nonsense.

"What next?"

"Let's dig in the sand," said Mr Silly.

"Good idea," said Little Miss Dotty.

So they went down to the beach and dug a big hole . . .

. . . and then filled it in!

"I did enjoy that," grinned Mr Nonsense.

"I'm hungry," said Little Miss Dotty. "What shall we eat?"

"Easy peasy," said Mr Nonsense, "sandwiches!"

And I'm sure you can guess what they did next.

That's right!

They put sand between slices of buttered bread and ate sand sandwiches!

Can you imagine anything more dotty?

After lunch they drew
in the sand . . .
with crayons!

And they sunbathed . . .
under umbrellas!

The sun was setting as they walked all the long way back to Little Miss Dotty's house and had supper together.

"We must do that again," said Little Miss Dotty.

"We must," agreed the other two.

And they got up from the table and went back to the beach!

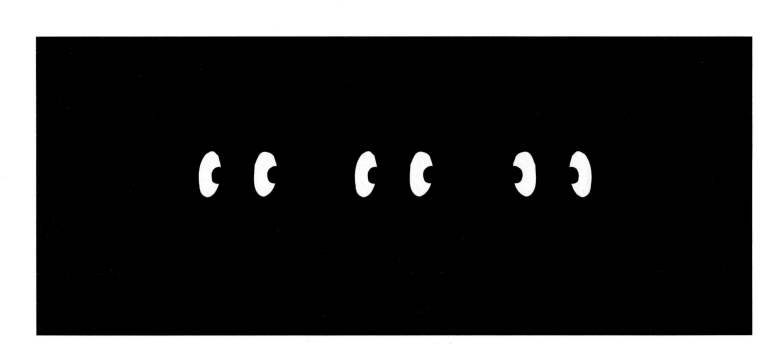

"It's very dark, isn't it?" said Little Miss Dotty.

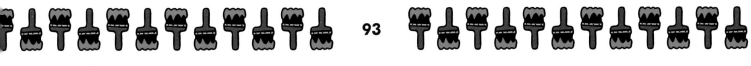

LITTLE MISS HELPFUL
and the green house

Little Miss Helpful loves to help.

So when Mr Slow says he wants

a greenhouse, she decides

to make his dream come true!

With a name like Helpful,

you would think that Little Miss Helpful would be helpful, wouldn't you?

Well, you'd be wrong.

She wanted to help people more than anything else in the world, but as hard as she tried, she always ended up being unhelpful.

One day, about a week ago, Little Miss Helpful was sitting on a bus on her way to town.

Mr Slow and Mr Happy were sitting in front of her having a conversation.

"I . . . wish . . . I . . . had . . . a . . . green . . . house . . . but . . . I . . . never . . . get . . . the . . . time . . . to . . . do . . . anything," said Mr Slow to Mr Happy.

It was a very slow conversation.

95

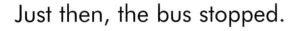
Just then, the bus stopped.

What Little Miss Helpful had just overheard had given her an idea.

She got off the bus.

And she walked across to Mr Nail's hardware store, and bought all the green paint that he had.

Then Mr Nail delivered all the green paint to Mr Slow's house.

I am sure you can guess what Little Miss Helpful had in mind. That's right.

She was going to surprise Mr Slow by helping him paint his house green.

How helpful of Little Miss Helpful!

Little Miss Helpful started to paint.

She painted all the walls.

She painted all the doors.

She painted the chimney
and the roof!

She even painted
all the windows.

The window
panes as well
as the frames!

When she had finished painting the house, she still had some paint left over.

So she painted the garage as well.

Outside and inside!

Little Miss Helpful was terribly pleased with herself.

She stood back to admire her handiwork.

It was then that Mr Slow arrived back home.

In the time it had taken Little Miss Helpful to paint his house, he had bought a loaf of bread.

He isn't called Mr Slow for nothing.

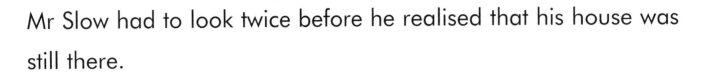

Mr Slow had to look twice before he realised that his house was still there.

"What . . . have . . . you . . . done?" he exclaimed.

"You said that you wanted a green house," said Little Miss Helpful, "so there you are."

"That's . . . not . . . what . . . I . . . meant. I . . . want . . . a . . . greenhouse," said Mr Slow.

"Exactly," said Little Miss Helpful. "And I painted your house green."

"No, I . . . want . . . the . . . sort . . . of . . . greenhouse . . . that . . . you . . . grow . . . tomatoes . . . in," explained Mr Slow, slowly.

"Oh . . ." said Little Miss Helpful.

". . . then what colour did you want your house to be?"

Mr Slow groaned a very slow groan. He could see it was going to be a very long afternoon.

Even for him!

LITTLE MISS SPLENDID
and the house with a view

Little Miss Splendid's house has
a splendid view apart from
her un-splendid neighbour, Mr Mean!
But things are about to change . . .

Little Miss Splendid

looked out of her very splendid window, set in her most splendid house, at her very splendid garden and smiled.

And then she frowned.

Little Miss Splendid looked out of her window every morning and every morning she smiled and then she frowned.

And what made her frown?

I'll tell you.

At the bottom of her garden on the other side of a small stream lived Mr Mean.

Unlike Little Miss Splendid's very large and most splendid house, Mr Mean's house is very small and very run down.

A not at all splendid house.

In fact, the most un-splendid house one could ever imagine.

Mr Mean was the sort of person who did not like spending money, especially on his house.

Little Miss Splendid was the complete opposite.

And she did not like having Mr Mean as a neighbour.

His house quite ruined her splendid view.

It was on this particular morning as she stood looking out of her window, that Little Miss Splendid had an idea.

She rang her builder, Mr Trowel.

"Hello," she said, "this is Little Miss Splendid. I would like you to build a wall for me. Come at once."

Mr Trowel was over within an hour and within a day, he had built a wall at the bottom of Little Miss Splendid's garden.

A high wall.

A wall that hid Mr Mean's house.

Now, Mr Mean also liked to look out of his window each morning.

He had a splendid view of Little Miss Splendid's extraordinarily splendid house.

And what made the view all the more splendid for Mr Mean was the fact that it hadn't cost him a penny.

109

Mr Mean was very unhappy when he looked out of his window the next day. All he could see was a high, red brick wall.

But, as he stood there looking out of his window, Mr Mean had an idea.

The next morning when Little Miss Splendid looked out of the window, she couldn't believe her eyes.

There was a huge hole in her beautiful wall and through the hole she could see Mr Mean's ramshackle house.

Little Miss Splendid was furious.

She rang Mr Trowel and by lunchtime, Mr Trowel had rebuilt the wall.

But the next morning, there was another hole in her wall.

And so it went on all week.

Over night, Mr Mean would knock a hole in the wall and the next day, Mr Trowel would come and repair it.

And then one morning, the whole wall had disappeared!

But not just the wall.

There was no sign of Mr Mean's house either!

"That's strange," said Little Miss Splendid to herself. She put on her best hat and went to investigate.

When she got down to where Mr Mean's house had been, she heard the sound of building coming from the other side of the hill. She climbed to the top of the hill.

And for the second time she couldn't believe her eyes.

There was Mr Busy putting the finishing touches to a house that looked liked hers, but was even more splendid!

113

"Looks good, doesn't it?" said a voice behind her.

It was Mr Mean.

"What . . . what . . . how?" spluttered Little Miss Splendid.

"It was all those bricks that gave me the idea," said Mr Mean and grinned. "All those free bricks!"

Little Miss Splendid didn't know what to say.

So she didn't say anything.

And she went home.

To her splendid house.

A splendid house, but no longer
the most splendid house!

LITTLE MISS TINY
just the right size

Little Miss Tiny decides to explore.
Being small is lots of fun
but she soon finds herself
in big, big, trouble!

Little Miss Tiny lives in a mouse hole in the dining room of Home Farm.

One day, she woke up early and decided to go exploring.

Exploring upstairs!

In all the time she had lived at Home Farm, she had never been upstairs.

Well, when you are as small as Little Miss Tiny, a staircase is like a mountain.

Little Miss Tiny started to climb the stairs.

She climbed, and she climbed, and she climbed some more.

All the way to the top.

It took her nearly the whole morning!

Everything was very quiet because everyone had gone out for the day.

She wandered through the bedrooms.

She explored the bathroom.

And then she discovered the nursery.

Lying on the floor was a box with a hook on the lid.

She lifted the hook . . .

. . . and got the fright of her life.

"Help!" she shrieked, and hid under the bed.

After a while, she plucked up courage and peeked out.

"You silly-billy," she said to herself, "it's only a jack-in-the-box."

She began to look around.

It was wonderful.

She said, "How do you do," to a very serious-looking soldier.

She tickled a teddy bear.

And climbed a tower of blocks.

It was from the top of the blocks that Little Miss Tiny saw the most wonderful sight she had seen in all her tiny life.

A doll's house!

Little Miss Tiny opened the front door and went in.

Everything was just the right size for her. The chairs, the table, the cups and even the stairs.

She went upstairs.

And lay down on the bed and closed her eyes.

She suddenly woke up with a start.

There, looking through the bedroom window of the doll's house, was the farm cat!

Little Miss Tiny didn't know what to do. How was she going to get back to her mouse hole?

She went downstairs and through a door.

The farm cat watched her through the windows.

She found herself in a garage on the side of the doll's house, and in the garage was a wind-up toy car.

The little car gave her an idea.

She turned the key on the car, wound it up and jumped in.

The little car took off like a rocket through the little garage doors and straight through the cat's legs!

The car and Little Miss Tiny raced across the carpet, out through the door and down the landing.

Little Miss Tiny laughed with glee.

And then realised she had laughed too soon.

The car shot over the top step of the stairs and out into space
and down . . .

and down . . .

and down . . .

Little Miss Tiny shrieked.

With a SPLASH! she landed in the cat's bowl of milk at the bottom of the stairs.

She rushed through the hall, ran across the dining room floor and back to the safety of her mouse hole.

"Phew! That was close!" she said, with a big sigh of relief.

Well, a big sigh of relief

for someone as tiny as Little Miss Tiny.

LITTLE MISS CONTRARY
all in a muddle

Little Miss Contrary always says
and does things the opposite to how
you would think. See what happens
when Mr Muddle comes to stay . . .

Little Miss Contrary lives in a place called Muddleland.

In Muddleland, hens live in cow barns, which works.

And cows live in chicken coops, which doesn't work!

Muddleland suits Little Miss Contrary down to the ground, or up to the sky, as they say in Muddleland.

When she goes into the butcher's and asks for apples, the butcher gives her a loaf of bread!

Which is what she had wanted all along.

Not so very long ago, Little Miss Contrary was having breakfast, at lunchtime, when the telephone rang.

Little Miss Contrary went to the front door, but of course there was no one there.

The phone rang again. She picked it up. The wrong way round. "Goodbye!" she shouted.

Everyone in Muddleland has to shout when they use the phone.

It was Mr Muddle on the phone.

Now you would think Mr Muddle also lived in Muddleland, wouldn't you? But he doesn't.

He wanted to, but got muddled-up and bought a house on the coast near Seatown.

However, each year he goes to Muddleland for his holidays and stays with Little Miss Contrary.

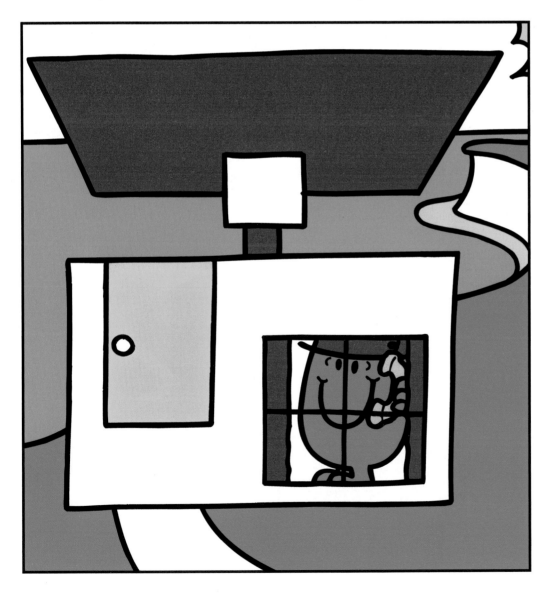

"I'd simply hate for you to come and stay. I'll see you last week. Hello!" finished Little Miss Contrary, and hung up the telephone.

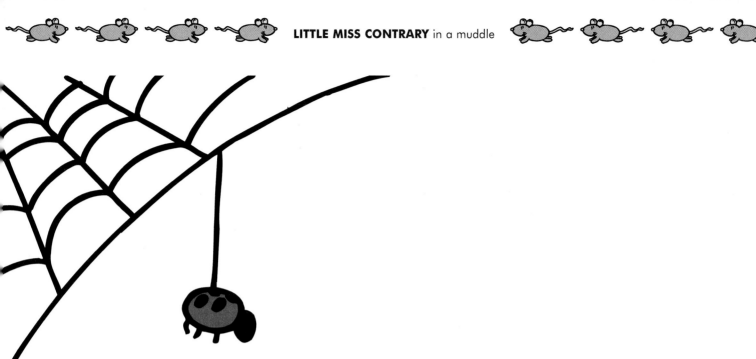

Little Miss Contrary looked around her.

"This house needs a good autumn-clean," she said to herself.

And, of course, what she meant was that her house needed a good spring-clean.

She polished
the carpets
and hoovered
the beds!

And she scrubbed
the television and
washed the plants!

In the middle of all this scrubbing and polishing and washing, Little Miss Contrary saw a cat.

Little Miss Contrary is terrified of cats.

Well, she isn't called Little Miss Contrary for nothing, is she?

With an "EEEEK!" she leapt on to a stool.

Poor Little Miss Contrary.

She was too frightened to get down off the stool.

And there she stayed.

All night long.

The next morning, there was a knock at the door.

"Go away!" called Little Miss Contrary, meaning 'Come in'.

Luckily, it was Mr Muddle on the other side of the door, so in he went.

"Oh, don't help me!" cried Little Miss Contrary. "There's a cat loose in the house!"

Mr Muddle understood completely.

"I don't know what to do," he said, and left.

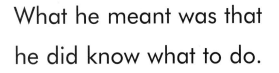
What he meant was that he did know what to do.

And in no time at all he returned with a mouse.

And the mouse, being a Muddleland mouse, chased the cat out of the house.

Little Miss Contrary made a saucer of tea and she and Mr Muddle settled down for a chat.

A chat that is much too muddling to write down here, and anyway, it's getting late now, and it's time to switch off the light and go to sleep.

Well it isn't really, but that is what Little Miss Contrary would have written if she was writing this story, but luckily she isn't.

You see, Little Miss Contrary gets everything the wrong way round.

She turns her lights off when it gets dark . . .

. . . and turns them on when she goes to bed!

Good morning!

LITTLE MISS NAUGHTY
and the Good Fairy

When Little Miss Naughty meets
the Good Fairy, things don't
turn out quite the way she expects.

Little Miss Naughty got up, stretched, opened her curtains and looked out of her window.

"What's that?" she said, peering more closely.

She went downstairs, out of the back door and down to the bottom of her garden.

"Look at that!" she cried. "It's a fairy ring!"

At her feet was a ring of mushrooms growing in the dewy grass.

"I wonder what happens if I step into the ring?" thought Little Miss Naughty.

And what happened was that she shrank to the size of a matchbox.

"Oh, help!" she wailed. "What do I do now?"

She looked around and noticed that there was a door in the stem of one of the mushrooms.

"I wonder what happens if I go through that door?" she asked herself.

And what happened was that she found herself in Fairyland!

On a hilltop, in the distance, was a glittering castle. Little Miss Naughty set off to see who lived there.

"Who are you?" asked a voice above her.

Startled, Little Miss Naughty looked up to see a fairy with gossamer wings hovering just above her head.

"I'm Little Miss Good," lied Little Miss Naughty.

"What a coincidence! I'm the Good Fairy. You must come and stay the night."

The Good Fairy waved her wand and whisked them up to her castle.

Little Miss Naughty could think of nothing but the mischief she might get up to if she was a fairy with her own magic wand and her own wings.

That night, Little Miss Naughty was very naughty. She stole the Good Fairy's wand!

She crept out of the castle and ran back to the magical wood. There she found a door in a tree which opened into the ring of mushrooms at the bottom of her garden.

As soon as she stepped out of the fairy ring, she grew back to her normal size.

Once Little Miss Naughty was safely inside her house, she looked at the wand in her trembling hand.

She closed her eyes, waved the wand and said, "Turn me into a fairy."

When she opened her eyes, she had a perfect pair of fairy wings.

She gave them a little flutter and felt herself rise off the floor.

"Oh, what fun I am going to have!" she cried.

The next day, she saw
Mr Bump walking along
the pavement.

She waved the magic wand
and a hole appeared in front
of Mr Bump and in he fell.

From her perch on a roof
high above, Little Miss
Naughty chuckled to herself.

But at that very moment,
a high wall fell across the
pavement just where Mr
Bump would have been
walking.

"Thank goodness I fell
into this hole," said
Mr Bump, peering up
the street.

Little Miss Naughty then found Farmer Barns looking at his field of corn.

With another chuckle, Little Miss Naughty waved the wand and the field of corn turned into a ploughed field.

But there in the middle was the farmer's dog who had been lost.

"Thank goodness the corn disappeared and I found Fido," said a relieved Farmer Barns.

Little Miss Naughty was very puzzled.

It seemed that as hard as she tried to be naughty, things kept turning out for the best.

She made it rain on Little Miss Sunshine, who could not have been happier because her tomatoes needed watering.

She created a mess in Little Miss Neat's front room. But she was overjoyed because she had Mr Messy coming for tea and she wanted to make him feel at home.

By the time Little Miss Naughty got home, she had never caused so much happiness in her life.

"This thing's no good," she said, throwing the wand on the table.

"That is where you are very wrong," said a voice.

Little Miss Naughty nearly jumped out of her skin.

It was the Good Fairy.

"That wand is all good because it is my wand. I hope that making so many people happy may have done you some good."

"So this will only make good things happen?" asked Little Miss Naughty.

"That's right."

"And it will never allow you to do anything naughty?"

"That's right."

"There is one more thing I need to know," said Little Miss Naughty.

"What is that?" asked the Good Fairy.

151

"Where does the Naughty Fairy live?"

LITTLE MISS STUBBORN
the wrong advice

Stubbornness can make life very
difficult as Little Miss Stubborn knows
only too well. Will a decision to listen
to other people's advice help her?

How stubborn is Little Miss Stubborn?

I'll tell you.

She was driving along the other day when she came to a sign which said, 'BRIDGE WASHED AWAY!'.

"Nonsense!" she cried. "If I want to drive along this road then I will!"

And she carried straight on . . .

. . . into the river!

SPLASH!

Well, she would, wouldn't she? There was no bridge.

That's how stubborn Little Miss Stubborn is.

The one thing she hates more than anything else in life is advice.

If you are as stubborn as her, advice is there to be ignored.

For instance, she always walks under ladders.

She never wears a hat when it's cold.

She always opens umbrellas indoors.

Not because she particularly wants to, but because she has been told that she shouldn't.

And needless to say, Little Miss Stubborn was fed up.

However, last Monday she met Little Miss Sunshine.

Little Miss Stubborn was covered in wet paint. The sign on the bench had read 'WET PAINT', but she had sat down anyway.

"Do you know what your problem is?" said Little Miss Sunshine. "You always ignore good advice. You ought to start listening to what people have to say, and save yourself a lot of trouble."

On the way home, Little Miss Stubborn thought about what Little Miss Sunshine had said.

And she thought about it over dinner.

And she stayed up all night thinking about it.

And by the morning, she had decided she would take Little Miss Sunshine's advice, which meant listening to everyone else's advice as well!

She set off into town, to go shopping.

The first person she met was Mr Wrong.

"Don't turn right at the end of the road, there's a hole in the ground," advised Mr Wrong.

Little Miss Stubborn was about to say, "Don't be ridiculous," when she remembered what she had decided.

"Thank you," she said.

When she got to the end of the road, she turned left and . . .

. . . fell down a hole!

BUMP!

Mr Wrong had got it wrong as usual.

The next day she took
Little Miss Dotty's advice
and used the hairdresser
she recommended.

Oh dear!

She took Mr Silly's advice on the best place to buy an umbrella.

She took Little Miss Scatterbrain's advice on directions to the beach.

And Mr Dizzy told her about his new short-cut to avoid the traffic.

Little Miss Stubborn was fed up.

Again.

At the end of the week, she met Little Miss Sunshine in the grocer's.

"Mind the . . ." began Little Miss Sunshine.

"Stop," said Little Miss Stubborn. "No more advice."

"But you're about to . . ."

"No!" said Little Miss Stubborn.

"Not another word!" demanded Little Miss Stubborn, who turned and . . .

. . . pointed to a sign.

"I know this is a slippery floor, but I want to go this way so I will."
And then she slipped over.

BUMP!

"You really are the most stubborn person I know,"
laughed Little Miss Sunshine.

"No I'm not!" said Little Miss Stubborn.

LITTLE MISS SUNSHINE
and the Wicked Witch

Little Miss Sunshine discovers a
Wicked Witch who is casting evil spells.
Can she put a stop to her nasty tricks?

Little Miss Sunshine

was going for a walk. It was rainy, but it takes a lot more than that to dampen Little Miss Sunshine's spirits.

In the distance, she saw Little Miss Bossy approaching.

"I will be nice to Little Miss Bossy," thought Little Miss Sunshine, "so she won't boss me around."

However, as she got closer, there was a bright flash and Little Miss Bossy turned into a bat!

A blue, very squeaky, bossy sort of a bat.

"How extraordinary!" exclaimed Little Miss Sunshine, as she watched Little Miss Bossy fly away.

But almost as extraordinary, was the cackling laugh she thought she heard coming from the clouds above.

The next day, the sun was out and there was not a cloud in sight. Little Miss Sunshine was wondering what had happened to Little Miss Bossy, when she saw Mr Rude walking towards her.

"I will be nice to Mr Rude," thought Little Miss Sunshine, "or he will be rude to me."

But at that moment, there was a bright flash and she discovered Mr Rude had turned into a toad.

A red, very rude, angry-looking toad.

And just like the day before, Little Miss Sunshine heard a cackling laugh. But this time it seemed to be coming from a tree.

On her walk the following day, Little Miss Sunshine had nearly reached Little Miss Dotty when there was another blinding flash.

Little Miss Dotty turned into a mouse!

A very confused, dotty, blonde-haired mouse.

When Little Miss Sunshine heard the same laugh, she ducked behind a bush and waited to see if she could find out who it came from.

Suddenly, with a rustle of leaves, a witch flew out.

A horrible hook-nosed, hairy, warty Wicked Witch, on a broomstick.

Little Miss Sunshine felt very afraid, but she bravely followed the Wicked Witch into Whispering Wood. There she found the Wicked Witch's ramshackle cottage.

Nervously, she crept up to the window and cautiously peered in.

The Wicked Witch was stirring revolting ingredients into a large, black cauldron hanging over a fire. She was muttering to herself and Little Miss Sunshine listened hard to hear what she was saying.

This is what she heard:

"Hubble, bubble,
Toil and trouble,
Eye of newt and hair of hog,
Early tomorrow morning,
Turn Little Miss Sunshine
into a dog!"

Little Miss Sunshine needed help and she needed it fast.

She tiptoed round to the front door and hopped on to the Wicked Witch's broomstick.

The broomstick rose up into the air with a wobbly Little Miss Sunshine perched on top.

Little Miss Sunshine knew exactly who would be able to help, so she rode the broomstick to Little Miss Magic's house.

"There's a Wicked Witch living in Whispering Wood," explained Little Miss Sunshine, when she arrived. She told Little Miss Magic what she had seen and what she had heard.

". . . and I'm going to be turned into a dog tomorrow morning!" she gasped.

"That's awful!" said Little Miss Magic. "But this is just the sort of problem that I like dealing with."

"I hoped you would say that," said Little Miss Sunshine.

"Now, I'll tell you what we are going to do," continued Little Miss Magic.

At sunrise, Little Miss Sunshine and Little Miss Magic knocked at the Wicked Witch's door.

She opened it and with a flash, her spell turned Little Miss Sunshine into a dog.

"Hee, hee, hee," cackled the Wicked Witch. "That worked like a dream."

It was then that Little Miss Magic turned the Wicked Witch into a cat!

A smelly, scraggy, black cat that suddenly found herself looking up at a scary yellow dog.

The Wicked Witch cat let out a screech and fled.

And, barking noisily, the Little Miss Sunshine dog chased the Wicked Witch cat far away. So she would never find her way back.

When Little Miss Sunshine returned, Little Miss Magic turned her back into her old self. She then turned Little Miss Bossy and Mr Rude back to normal as well.

Little Miss Dotty took a lot longer to find as she was hidden in a mouse hole, and she seemed not to have noticed that anything had happened.

"Are you feeling all right?" asked Little Miss Sunshine, after Little Miss Magic had said a few magic words.

"Why, of course I am," said Little Miss Dotty. "Why shouldn't I?"

"Oh, no reason," said Little Miss Sunshine, winking at Little Miss Magic.

"Although," said Little Miss Dotty, twitching her nose, "I really fancy a nice piece of . . ."

". . . cheese!"

LITTLE MISS TROUBLE
and the Mermaid

When Little Miss Trouble goes to Seatown,
she decides to spend her holiday
causing trouble. But then she meets a
Mermaid who has other ideas . . .

The trouble with Little Miss Trouble is that she is always causing trouble. Like when she met Mr Greedy.

"Do you know that they are giving away ice creams around the corner?" she asked him.

"Really?" cried Mr Greedy, and raced off to get some.

What he did not know was that workmen had dug up the pavement.

Mr Greedy fell right down the hole. THUMP!

Little Miss Trouble thought this was very funny but Mr Greedy did not.

Now, the trouble with making trouble is that sometimes it can catch up with you.

And that is what happened when Little Miss Trouble went to Seatown.

Her first two days in Seatown were great fun for her, but no fun for anybody else!

She splashed Little Miss Splendid, and blamed Little Miss Chatterbox.

Little Miss Trouble kicked sand all over Mr Strong and then blamed Mr Sneeze . . . who Mr Strong buried in sand up to his nose!

On her third day in Seatown, Little Miss Trouble decided to go fishing with Mr Muddle and Little Miss Bossy. The three of them rowed out to sea and set up their fishing rods.

Little Miss Trouble was trying to think of the best way to cause trouble when she felt something tug on her fishing line.

"I've caught a fish!" she cried, excitedly.

Then there was a much stronger tug. A tug so strong that it pulled her right out of the boat!

Not only did it pull her out of the boat, it pulled her down into the sea.

Something, or someone, grabbed her foot and dragged her deeper and deeper.

It was not until she reached the bottom of the sea that she discovered who had caught her.

It was a mermaid!

"There is someone who wishes to see you," said the Mermaid to a flabbergasted Little Miss Trouble.

181

"Take me back!" demanded Little Miss Trouble.

"Later," said the Mermaid. "Now, follow me."

The Mermaid took Little Miss Trouble's hand and led her across the seabed.

After a short while, they came to a coral reef.

"Where are you taking me?" asked Little Miss Trouble.

"You are about to find out," replied the Mermaid.

In the middle of the reef was a circle of sand and a coral throne.

Sitting on the throne was the Mermaid Queen.

"I have brought Little Miss Trouble, Your Highness," said the Mermaid.

"So you are the person who has been causing so much trouble on my beach and in my sea!" said the Mermaid Queen. "It is time you learnt to behave yourself!"

"But it wasn't me!" exclaimed Little Miss Trouble. "It was Little Miss Chatterbox and Mr . . ."

To Little Miss Trouble's surprise, the word 'sneeze', which she had meant to say, came out as a bubble. And every time she tried to say it, the same thing happened, until there was a stream of bubbles coming out of her mouth!

"It is no good blaming other people," said the Mermaid Queen. "From now on, every time you try to make trouble, all that you will get for your trouble is bubbles! You may go back to the beach now."

184

The Mermaid led Little Miss Trouble to the edge of the coral reef, where a dolphin was waiting.

"This dolphin will take you back to Seatown. Do not forget what the Queen said," warned the Mermaid.

Little Miss Trouble rode the dolphin back to the beach.

The beach was crowded and as Little Miss Trouble watched the dolphin's fin as it swam away, an idea struck her.

"There's a . . . !" she shouted, but instead of the word 'shark', which she had meant to shout to scare everyone, bubbles came out of her mouth.

Everyone on the beach gave her a very odd look.

Feeling very foolish, Little Miss Trouble went back to her hotel.

The next morning, down on the beach, she found Little Miss Sunshine sunbathing. She crept up behind her and dropped her ice cream on her.

"Eek!" screamed Little Miss Sunshine, leaping up in surprise. "Who did that?"

"It was . . ." began Little Miss Trouble.

She was about to say, 'Mr Rush', but I am sure you know what came out instead.

Lots of bubbles!

"How could you!" cried Little Miss Sunshine, and threw what was left of the ice cream at Little Miss Trouble.

All Little Miss Trouble could do was blow bubbles.

And so it went on. Every time she tried to cause trouble, the same thing happened.

By the end of the week, Little Miss Trouble had given up and had started building sandcastles instead.

She became so good at building sandcastles that she won the sandcastle competition! She was very excited, until she discovered what the prize was.

A year's supply of bubble bath!

LITTLE MISS WHOOPS
always having accidents

Little Miss Whoops drops things
and is always knocking things over.
When she visits her brother, Mr Bump,
things immediately start to go wrong . . .

Little Miss Whoops is

one of those people who has accidents all of the time.

She has lots of little accidents, like when she drops the eggs!

Whoops!

And big accidents, like when she painted her bedroom and tripped over the paint pot!

Whoops!

Every morning when she makes her cup of tea, she spills the milk, tips over the sugar bowl, drops the tea bag, breaks the biscuits, knocks her cup across the table and has to start again. Whoops!

Some days it can take hours before she leaves the house.

Little Miss Whoops really is the most accidental person in the world . . . well not quite.

Little Miss Whoops has a brother, Mr Bump. He is just like her, if not worse, but that is another story. (Which you may have read.)

Each year, Little Miss Whoops goes to visit her brother for a week.

She set off last Tuesday.

This Tuesday, Mr Bump looked at his clock.

Which was on the ground where he had just knocked it over.

His sister was a whole week late!

192

And why was she late?

A whole chapter of accidents, of course!

While her train was waiting at a station, she tripped and fell out of the train.

Whoops!

And then she somehow or other tripped and fell into a lorry, which took her to Seatown.

Whoops!

Where, somehow or other she fell into a boat which took her to another country.

Whoops!

She had to wait nearly a week to get another boat back . . .

. . . and another lorry . . .

. . . and another train.

Little Miss Whoops was exhausted when she finally reached her brother's house.

"I thought you were coming last week?" said Mr Bump. "It must have been a long trip."

"It was!" said Little Miss Whoops.

"Would you like a cup of tea?" offered Mr Bump.

And you know what that involved don't you?

They spilt the milk, tipped over the sugar bowl, dropped the tea bags, broke the biscuits and knocked the tea all over the table!

What a mess!

Whoops!

"Oh! Look at the time," cried Little Miss Whoops, knocking over the clock. "I've got to go if I'm to catch my train home!"

She grabbed her suitcase and rushed out of the door.

"Goodbye," she called.

"Goodbye," called back Mr Bump. "See you next year!"

Mr Bump waved until she had rounded the corner.

Then he closed the door, but as he did, the door
handle came off in his hand!

"Whoops!" said Mr Bump.

LITTLE MISS BAD

is not good

Little Miss Bad is always doing naughty
things and worst of all, she lies!
How will they get her to start telling the truth?

Little Miss Sunshine looked out of the window and thought back on all the things that had happened in the last week.

Lots of things.

Lots of bad things.

Some things were just a little bit bad.

Mr Uppity's tennis racquet strings were swapped for spaghetti.

And the cream in Mr Greedy's cream buns was replaced with toothpaste.

Some things were really quite bad.

Little Miss Splendid's shower covered her with ink.

203

And someone had painted cracks on the walls of Mr Worry's house.

Mr Worry was so worried that his house might fall down, he had moved into his garden shed.

Some things were really very bad indeed!

Someone had sawn Mr Forgetful's car in half. Fortunately, Mr Forgetful did not get upset. He thought that he must have forgotten the other half and left it at home!

And someone had sneaked into Little Miss Neat's house while she was on holiday and left all the taps running.

Little Miss Neat did get upset.

Nobody knew who had done all these things, but Little Miss Sunshine had a very good idea who was behind it all.

"Little Miss Bad," she murmured to herself.

Little Miss Bad was not good.

Far from it.

In fact, about as far as you can get, which is a long way.

But how to catch Little Miss Bad? This was the question that Little Miss Sunshine was turning over in her mind.

Then she had a very clever idea.

The next day a poster appeared in the Town Square.

It announced a 'Grand Competition' to discover the most mischievous, naughty or bad trick that had been played in the last week. First prize was a fabulous holiday!

"How easy," said Little Miss Bad to herself. "That holiday is as good as mine."

The day of the Grand Competition dawned.

By midday, a large crowd had gathered by the stage in the middle of the square.

Little Miss Sunshine called for quiet.

"Each contestant," she explained, "will come up on stage and describe their entry and then the panel of judges will decide upon a winner. First up, is Little Miss Bad!"

Little Miss Bad could not wait to get on stage.

She was so excited.

She had spent all the previous night trying to pick her worst or best trick, depending on how you looked at it, but she had not been able to decide.

So she described them all. From Mr Uppity's tennis racquet strings all the way through to Little Miss Neat's wet house.

She described them in great detail.

She was so carried away she failed to notice that the crowd had fallen silent. It was only when she had finished that she saw the expressions on everyone's faces.

Little Miss Sunshine was the only person in the

square with a smile on her face, a rather smug smile, and it suddenly occurred to Little Miss Bad just what she had been tricked into doing.

"I-I-I was only j-j-joking," she stammered.

"Anything more to say?" said Little Miss Sunshine.

Little Miss Bad looked very ashamed. "I'm very sorry," she said.

210

Little Miss Bad had learnt her lesson that day.

The lesson continued for a number of weeks as it took her a long time to repair all the damage and clean Little Miss Neat's house.

Mr Forgetful's car will never look quite the same. Luckily he can't remember what it looked like in the first place.

But nothing she had to do was half as bad as those moments standing on the stage with the crowd glaring at her.

It was a very long time before she even thought of doing anything bad.

And the same could be said of one other person that day.

Mr Mischief. He slipped away from the crowd and slunk off home, where he breathed a very deep sigh of relief!

LITTLE MISS SCARY
loves to scare people

Little Miss Scary scares everyone she meets!
Who will help to stop Little Miss Scary
from frightening all her neighbours?

Little Miss Scary

lived near the top of a mountain in a house called Spooky Cottage.

When it was dark she would creep into the valley below, making sure that nobody saw her.

There she would wait very quietly until somebody came along.

And when that somebody did, she would tiptoe up behind them, open her mouth wide and shout . . .

"BOO!"

215

And do you know why Little Miss Scary did this?

For fun.

You see, she loved to scare people more than anything else in the world.

And she was very good at it.

She scared them stiff.

 **"BOO!"**

She scared them out of their wits.

"BOO!"

She even scared them right out of their socks.

"BOO!"

About a week ago, Mr Noisy went to see his friend Mr Jelly.

Mr Noisy was worried because he hadn't heard from his friend for ages.

When he got to Mr Jelly's house, he knocked on the door.

Spookily, the door swung open by itself.

"Hello," called Mr Noisy as softly as he could, which for you or I would have been a shout.

Then he heard a chattering noise coming from the bedroom.

Mr Noisy found Mr Jelly hiding under his bed, his teeth chattering in fear.

"Whatever's the . . ." began Mr Noisy, and then remembered himself. "Whatever's the matter, Mr Jelly?"

"It's . . . it's . . . L-L-Little Miss S-S-Scary," chattered Mr Jelly, trembling in fear. "Sh-sh-she keeps jumping out and shouting 'b-b-b-boo' at me."

219

 **LITTLE MISS SCARY** loves to scare people

Mr Noisy made
Mr Jelly a cup of
tea, calmed him
down and told
him what they
were going to do.

 **LITTLE MISS SCARY** loves to scare people

Just as it was getting
dark, they hid behind
a bush beside the
lane that led up to
Mr Jelly's house.

They waited until they
saw Little Miss Scary's
shadowy figure
creeping past them.

Then Mr Noisy and Mr Jelly crept out from their hiding place, tiptoed up behind Little Miss Scary and, at the top of their voices, shouted . . .

"BOO!"

Now, the top of Mr Noisy's voice is a very loud place indeed.

So loud that Little Miss Scary leapt five feet in the air and when she came down she ran for her life.

She didn't stop running until she was hidden under her bed. In her bedroom. In Spooky Cottage. At the top of the mountain.

"I don't think you'll be seeing much of her for a long while, Mr Jelly," chuckled Mr Noisy. "Mr Jelly? Mr Jelly . . . ?"

But there was no sign of Mr Jelly, either.

Mr Noisy chuckled again and walked back to
Mr Jelly's house. To have a look under Mr Jelly's bed!

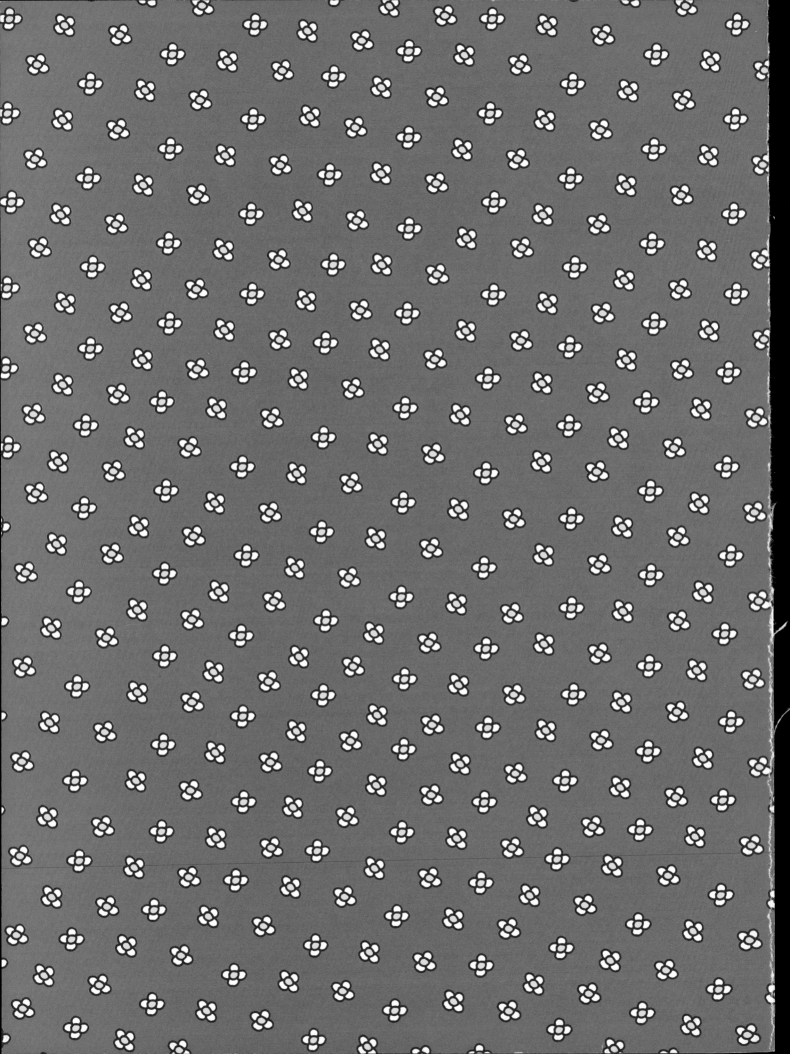